Andrew Masseurs is a creatively restless spirit. While spending over twenty years creating music, four albums and an EP, he found himself inexplicably focused on writing one day on holiday. The result, his first exciting novella, *A Day in the Life, Book One*.

Andrew is a loving husband and father to four kids living in the beautiful country that is New Zealand. Living a busy life, running his own business, he is now busy writing book's one, two and three of the *A Day in the Life* series.

To my loving wife, Hana.
My support and soulmate.

A Day in the Life (Novella)

A Day in the Life Series, Book One
Andrew Masseurs

Copyright © 2024 by Andrew Masseurs.

All rights reserved.

No part of this publication may be reproduced, distributed, or transmitted in any form or by any means, including photocopying, recording, or other electronic or mechanical methods, without the prior written permission of the publisher, except as permitted by U.S. copyright law.

The story, all names, characters, and incidents portrayed in this production are fictitious. No identification with actual persons (living or deceased), places, buildings, and products is intended or should be inferred.

ISBN 9 789694 492247 (Paperback)

ISBN 9 789694 492254 (Hardcover)

ISBN 9 789694 492261 (ePub e-book)

ISBN 9 798823 483681 (Audiobook)

Book Cover by Chris Era

Edition 2 2024. First Published 2023

Andrew Masseurs®

www.andrewmasseurs.com

Thank you to my wife and family for your constant inspiration and support as I create. To my mum and dad who made me who I am (thank you and miss you) To the A Day in the Life book series A-Team: Chris Era, for your amazing cover artwork, Jessica Hay for your diligent editing and lastly, David Piper for your passionate work on the A Day in the Life audiobook. You are all the window into this world and I can't thank you enough.

Chapter One

Happiness

What a day I've had. Perfection would be a good description. Awakening with no ailments, no problems, no falsehoods. It's as if youth had come back to reclaim its heyday. Being the ripe old age of 48, I am well past the unhinged exuberance of super-heroism, when nothing could hurt me, and it seemed, nothing did, till my calves gave in and would pinch every other month. But today, I feel good. A quick search on my fitness app, as I change the settings to 250m, and proceed to sprint the distance, with a drill sergeant telling me I'm doing a shit job, and to pick up my ideas. I love this app. Or indeed, I love it on a good day. I proceed to do 10 x 250 metre sprints, with a walk in between, and my stomach doesn't feel so big. I have been training for what seems like most of my life. I have the discipline to train, cause I love the results, and positive vibes that come as a result, but not the discipline to take it to a perfect body or diet. With age comes an understanding, I feel that balance is more important for happiness than going too far one way or the other. As a result, breakfast is tampered down to something healthy. Oats, fruit and milk. Bringing the energy back to full bars, I look forward to what the day will bring. My daughter wakes with questions and enthusiasm. I love the day she was born. She is everything right about the world, and her questions make me proud and filled with excited wisdom. I try to answer without true knowledge, but the best I can do at the time. I do not read much and my mind is only aware of what interests me at the moment, but when added together, sometimes, it is worthwhile. She listens to me as a daughter who loves her father. We laugh and smile at our efforts, before talking about our day ahead, and what it entails.

Mother comes in with thunder and giggles. Carrying a load of freshly dried washing, she is whistling her way through another morning. She has already made breakfast for everyone but herself, and has done most chores that would take anyone else a day at least. Forever positive, we talk about last night's TV series, and the latest happenings. It is a beautiful day outside, with a brisk, calming breeze. One of those days that you wish not to lose, and after my run, I am eager to realise.

There is something about a holiday that energises the soul. It has been a long time between drinks, and the sound of roaring waves and wind, makes the heart stronger, and full of ideas. I need to do it more often, but costs and work make it all too difficult. I am far from wealthy, and work has always been needed, to keep us above board. I see houses here that make me think of mortgages and carefree days away from the hustle of town. If only my job could be done from a beach house, with the sea as my inspiration. I am sure my life would be longer and happier in this perfect coastal location. My daughter wishes to go for a walk. Mother comes with and we hold hands in cheesy rhythms as we enjoy the summer walk. Kids are playing on the beach. Laughter is heard from far away as picnics and bodyboards are enjoyed.

I think to myself, *could this day be any better?* We stop at the four square for ice cream. Burnt bodies are everywhere, with people who should know better showing way too much flesh. Everyone is polite and smiling, as the day has also absorbed into their manners. I grab the triple scoop, with chocolate covering, knowing it is a mistake as soon as I step out into the sun. Mother and daughter laugh, as I lose the melting mess that was once a biscuit-flavoured, triple scooped wonder. The day is filled with swims and laziness, books and food. As I said, a perfect day with my loved ones.

Now, they are gone.

I awoke, after too much drink, with a dry taste in my mouth. Silly not to drink water before I went to bed. I check the iPhone for emails and Facebook crap, before losing 10 minutes and remembering I wanted to check the time. It's 8:30 am, way past my usual wake up time of 6 am. The sea is making its usual noise, and I feel comforted. Though I feel a little worse for wear, my first thought is exercise. *What should I do today?* Yesterday was sprints, today should be distance. Mixing it up is a sure way to stave off boredom. Once clothes are found from the holiday piled mess, I quickly dress and walk into the hallway. The holiday house I've rented is modest. Nothing special, but it works. Nothing like the multi-million dollar complexes that work along the foreshore. *If only!* I think to myself. Walking into the small kitchen, I notice no one is up. After last night's antics, I decided they're all tired, so I let the sergeant drill me into pain, as the fitness app fires me on my run.

While running, a curious thing occurs to me. The streets are silent. No cars whizz past me. No kids running and playing. No walkers or runners to nod my head to. No one to ignore or ignore me as I run past them. It is strange, but it is Sunday after all. Ha! I am proud to be the only one making the effort on this quiet morning. I double my efforts for 10 metres, before going slower than before. I arrive back home feeling so much better and eager to see my beautiful daughter, as she jumps at me with more questions, and makes the day full of excited life. But no one is awake still. The house is quiet. The door I left open hasn't been touched. I make myself bacon, eggs and mushrooms. A welcome reward after the hefty distance travelled. Coffee is just instant. No special coffee machines for my taste buds, and I know no different, as it has not been a staple of my diet. Nevertheless, I enjoy this unprofessional breakfast, and wait for stirrings in the household.

11 am and no one up. After watching another episode I wasn't supposed to (my wife will kill me) I investigate the house. Main room empty. Mother isn't there. The bed we slept in is not made. I quickly make it, hating mess, and check the bathroom, no sign. Walking down the old hallway, I knock on daughter's door. No answer. I walk in, and notice an unusual mess. Strange, she is up,

and her room is not perfect. Most days, I arrive back home to find her perfect room made up. Like something out of a magazine. She respects her place, and feels good about keeping things tidy. *Where did she get that from?* I'm so proud of her, but again, unusual for her to leave this room unkept. I make the room up, and look forward to her arriving home with a heartfelt thank you. She must have been in a hurry. *Maybe she's exercising?* She is like me in that; she loves to keep herself fit. I like to think I have inspired her, but this is a father's foolish thinking. She is her own inspiration. *Maybe they went shopping?* Holidays inspire money spending, unlike anything seen before or after. Gone are the worries of bill paying. That will take care of itself, once reality sets in. Reality is at least five days away, so let's not think about that, shall we? I settled in for one more episode. Mother loves to watch episodes while I'm away. She knows it pains me, but she can't help but finish a season when it's very good. I pretend to be angry, but it's all false bravado, as there's no way I could be angry with my beautiful wife, who smiles back at me with her perfect face. *How did I ever manage to snap her up?* I ask myself. I endeavour to catch up with her, but as I do, she is already watching something else. We usually enjoy things together. I am influenced by a lot of what she says. More than she realises, or that I'd tell her. She is, after all, my wife.

2 pm, and no sign of my family. I am starting to wonder, but it is not unusual for them to disappear for hours. Shopping, visiting, or getting the latest book for daughter dearest to read. I phone mother and hear the iPhone ringing in our bedroom. Strange, she left it behind. I try daughter, and also hear her phone ringing next to her now made bed. Stranger still, that daughter doesn't have her phone with her. They must have been in a hurry. I decide to not lose the day.

Swearing under my breath that they did not take me along, I decide to go for a swim, and at least enjoy myself as they are. Walking down to the beach, I notice a quiet stillness, that is more unusual for the afternoon than it was for the morning. I hear no kids screaming. No picnics being enjoyed. Upon walking onto the expanse that is the open beach, I notice no one is enjoying this perfect day. No hint of a breeze, and the sun sitting at a warm 26 degrees. It is hot, and the water will be at its best a cooling temperature. *Where is everybody?* This is now weird. Did I miss something? Was there a special event I missed on the news? Surely people would still come for a swim on such a perfect day. I shrug, drop my towel, and enjoy the coolness of the water. The beaches here are cold and brown. Nothing beautiful about the water. Nothing like the pacific countries you may holiday in. The sand is fine, but definitely not golden and soft as some paradises I have visited. Murky and suspicious, I try not to take in any water. It is still nice to sink under though, and let the weightlessness lift you into a dreamless state. Feeling refreshed and happy, I leave the water and dry myself warm. Again the beaches are empty. As the wind becomes stronger, I notice no wind surfers. The waves are starting to form, but there is no sign of kids with bodyboards to take advantage of the swell. I look at houses that lift above the sand dunes. Checking into windows that are large and shaded, I notice no movement. *Must be a coincidence,* I think. Walking home, I laugh at the chance that I have not seen anyone all day. *What are the percentages that this could have happened to someone, the odds? Crazy!* I think. Can't wait to tell the girls on their return.

4 pm, and still no sign. I decide to surprise my family with a meal made on the BBQ. Chicken, slow cooked, salted and peppered to the best of my YouTube-inspired brilliance. I'm not the best when it comes to cooking. No training per say, but enough of a creative spark, that I can get away with following a recipe, or a remark made on a cooking show. I also tend to ask questions, when I see something that I need to recreate. Salad is something summery. Lettuce, apples and grapes with tomatoes; light and tasty. A light caesar salad dressing added to the mix and we are ready to go. I wish I could text the wife to bring a dessert, but she didn't take her phone, god dammit. *Is it too early to drink? Not too early,* I think, and cooking is always so much more fun with a slight buzz

to carry you through the monotony of cutting veggies.

After my fourth craft beer, the chicken is starting to be forgotten, and a slight burned tinge is appearing on the skin, which is now stuck to the hot plate. Should have listened to Arnold. Don't bake drunk. I've set the slightly wonky picnic table with three plates. Everything is now perfect. I've had enough beer, and don't want to appear drunk to my girls returning from there day trip. I make myself a coffee and settle in for another episode of the latest watch.

7 pm, I fell asleep during the second episode of whatever I was watching, and am now hungry and worried. Covering the food I prepared, I look out onto the street. Empty and quiet. I have not seen anyone all day. Okay, now warning bells are going off. I decide to go for a drive, and investigate the rest of the city. I leave a hastened note on the table. 'Cooked you dinner. Hope you had a great day. Love you both. Popped out for a bit.' Hopping in the smaller Baby Yoda car, as we call it, and drive into the quiet city. By quiet, I mean dead quiet. I

did not pass one car. Nor did a car pass me going the other way. All house lights seemed to be off. The street lights were going, but apart from that, it was dark. As I passed shops, some lights were on, most were off. I decided to get some petrol, and ask the attendant what the hell was going on. I drove into a quiet Caltex station. The lights were on and the shop seemed to be open. I pressed fill on the buttons, and proceeded to fill up the tank. Walking into the shop, I saw no one. I screamed out for someone, but nothing. *Crazy,* I thought. *This is fuckin' crazy.* I don't normally swear, but on this occasion, it felt deserved. My daughter would normally say, 'Hey, hey calm down' after a remark like that. My wife would probably swear with me. I'm starting to miss them, and their quirks. *What is going on?* It's like some silly sci-fi movie. I try to work the machine behind the till to pay. I've had some experience in retail, but this all reads like Egyptian. Instead, I leave a note saying I tried, and leave my phone number.

Cameras are in operation, and I don't want to be that guy with his photo on the local Facebook community page. I walk out onto the empty lot, and sit on the bench by the blinking sign. Not a soul to be seen. Not a sound. Come to think of it, I haven't even heard a dog bark. I hop back in the car and speed back home. I'm now sweating and starting to feel sick. I switch the radio that is normally off, between stations to hear something, anything... nothing. Nothing but static. I slam my foot on the accelerator, and fly through the quiet night, not caring if the police stop me. I know now, there are probably no police.

Chapter Two

Solo

I walk into the quiet, empty, dark house. I turn on the lights that now seem to be the only lights on in the whole street. Running to the TV, I quickly run through the apps on the Apple TV. Everything is working. *Strange,* I think to myself, *but maybe not.* Most apps are probably working on an automatic setting. I check the live feeds. Channel one, channel three, nothing. No broadcast. Okay, now I'm panicking. I grab my iPhone, and proceed to call family. My mum, my brothers, my sister, no answer. Only messages. I leave messages for everyone. I ring contacts, and business contacts. No answer. Finally, I try the police, and receive a voice message with choices. It fills me with some familiarity and optimism, but not much. I try a choice which does not get answered.

For the rest of the night I sit in the lounge on the old three seater, looking at a turned off TV set. Listening to the ocean and the waves roaring. Oh, to hear a voice.

It's been seven days now. I have not seen a person, nor an animal. I'm still in the holiday house I was supposed to vacate three days ago. I'm hoping I will wake, and my wife and daughter will be there for me, as if nothing happened. I've heard nothing, nor seen anything that tells me anyone is alive. No vehicles, no planes, no trains. I miss my family. Each day, I travel a little further than the last. Hoping to see someone or find something that'll tell me what's happened. But nothing. I leave notes for things I have taken in shops I have shopped at. The power has still been going in most places. Food seems to be refrigerated, so for the time being, I am fine. I'm trying to stay calm, and rationally come up with something to explain all this. Work was on my mind for a second, before I thought, *what are you thinking? There's no one fucking here! Idiot.* I procured a couple dozen craft beers, and some smokes for the evening. I don't smoke, unless I drink heavily. Something brought on from my youth. I drank almost all the beer. I smoked most of the packet. I watched old movies on Netflix, and reminisced. I was both sad and drunk. It was like a sign. A goodbye signal to my past life, and an end to what I knew would not change. Everyone was gone. My beautiful family was not coming back.

I woke feeling pasty and horrible. The beach was loud in my head. I hate the day after. I knew I could not carry on this way and survive if I did not create some discipline in myself. Some routine, to keep me occupied. I decided that I'd start a diary of sorts tomorrow. Some creative writing to keep my thoughts in check. It's maddening, thinking to myself and sometimes answering. The holiday house is now over. My family is gone. They are not returning. I've decided to go back home. My wife has a huge calendar in the entrance way. I'll go back there, and tick off each day. A sign that I am alive and well should they come back. I've also written a list of things to learn. Power and electricity. How long will they operate without human help? Most expiration dates on dairy foods are quickly coming near. Milk and other foods will be going bad. I'd have to research what will last, and what I can use in the future. Petrol is something I might also need to start hoarding. Once the power goes, will the petrol stop pumping? So much to think about and work out. I also can't get rid of the sadness. I miss my wife and her laugh. I miss my daughter and her questions. Life is worthless without them.

Chapter Three

Home

I ARRIVE HOME TO an unsurprisingly empty house. The house is still as tidy as I left it. Just a deafening silence that fills the air. Damp, humid air envelopes me, as I open the windows and breathe the fresh air deeply. I sit on the breakfast seat by the bench, looking at the kitchen for what seems an age. My thoughts fall back to the day we left. Arguing about nothing in particular. Where the bags were kept, I seem to recall. The wife, as per usual, was taking care of all the real necessities. While I was trying to leave the house looking like some expensive motel, so we would feel good walking into a clean house on our return. "We don't have time," she said. I've lost her for all time it seems. I wish I could get that time back. The kitchen is now dark, and quiet. The open windows have brought in a cold chill, which wakes me and forces me to move and put on more clothes. I walk past my daughter's room as I near the master bedroom. The door is ajar, showing her perfectly kept room. The neatness breaks my heart, and I collapse, bellowing in the noiseless air. My tears and screaming can be heard echoing down the empty streets. The agony of losing my closest two has finally hit home. I don't think I stopped for most of the night.

I woke up to a damp pillow and sore eyes. Stung by the sorrow of this quiet empty home. My first thought is my wife would not want me to be this way and my daughter would already have ideas to keep the days ordered. I smile at the thought of her telling me what to do. All of fourteen and wise beyond her years. For the first week, I tick off the calendar each day and venture out into town to grab food and cans. I store everything neatly and ordered in the garage. As a thought, it might be easier for me to stay by a supermarket, but the thought lingers that my family might yet come home, so home is where I stay. Still no sight or sound of anyone or anything. I haven't noticed a bird or insect. It's almost as if every living thing on the face of the Earth has just vanished. I think about how the world would survive without animals to care and recycle it into full bloom. I think about this for all of two minutes before moving on to organising my days.

Without work, I now have time to start each morning with a workout at the local Gym. Takes about 45 minutes, and I've found my body is reacting faster and growing stronger due to the rest I have after the workouts. I'm able to take a nap in the afternoon, and sleep a good eight hours at night. I've set up the house with the latest appliances. Our dryer sucked, so I grabbed a super commercial dryer that dries in half the time with double the load. My TV is now an 80 inch 8k beast, with 7.1 surround sound. The neighbourhood has never heard *Star Wars* like this before.

It is a good thing and puts a little smile on my face for a little while anyway. I keep myself busy but am now starting to feel depressed, with little or no contact and just my memories to keep me going.

Today, I ventured up the motorway. It is now starting to look all very familiar. Some cars have been left smack bang in the centre. It looks like no one had a choice in what they were doing when they left the earth. Some cars veered into traffic. Some to the side of the road. The damage was quite significant. I dart in between the cars, becoming more and more familiar with the set up each time I travel this way. It has been over two months since the disappearance. A full beard has enveloped my unkempt face. The Ford Mustang GT-500 effortlessly powers me through the onslaught. A thrilling noise grunts my coming arrival. I can't get enough of this powerful car. The music is connected to my iPhone, and a selection of my favourite tunes rings out. I'm on my way back to the holiday home we had stayed in. My second visit. I go back in case my family have appeared. The calendar at home has been ticked off for the number of days I am away, and a fresh note left in case they arrive home. It's a crazy habit now, but it keeps me sane.

I enter the summer town, and it is now starting to look a little overgrown. Lawns are wild, and flowers are escaping as houses are becoming small jungles. How quickly absence creates anarchy. Cracks in the road are growing weeds, and cars that were smashed on the side of the road are now invaded by bushes. One truck has a sign on the back in large letters spelling home removal. I think to myself *that truck could be handy for moving items* when I notice my wife walking past the back of the truck looking angelic. *Wait! My wife…* bang! I smash into the back of a pickup truck, left in the middle of the road. The airbag blows and saves my impact. I'm unconscious for what seems like days.

My head hurts. My hand smears blood across my forehead, as I try to raise my head. The pain in my neck says I've done some damage. The fact I can get out of the car tells me I'm okay. *It's early morning,* I think. I've been out for what seems like

12 hours. Must have really hurt myself. The car is a write-off. The front is smashed in, coming off second best to a rather large pickup truck. *Time to pick something better*, I think to myself. Though the Mustang will be hard to beat, I look around. Shit! My wife. It comes back to me. I saw her! Clear as day. Walking away, almost floating across the road by the truck. She was a vision, beautiful, smiling almost. Wearing different clothes. She looked healthy. She looked good. She's alive! But why would she leave? She would've seen me, surely? I was right across the road. She looked at me. The crash. It was so loud. Am I crazy? Was she even there? I limp across the road. Stumbling around the truck. Looking up and down the overgrown street. Nothing, no one. The sun is starting to warm the cold night chill off my body as I check the next five houses, both ways, looking for signs of my wife. Quiet and empty. I limp over back to the car. I press the horn for long ten second bursts. The quiet streets echo the horn's blast. I wait for what seems like an hour. Pressing the horn and waiting. No one comes. Maybe I am going crazy.

In the far distance, I hear a clicking noise. Six or so evenly spaced clicks. Low and unearthly. I've never heard anything like it before. I pause. The quiet surrounds me. *My imagination,* I think. My mind drifts to the version of my wife. I decide to stay at the old holiday house we were staying in. I will scout the town for any possible signs of my wife. For any signs of life. If she is here, I will find her.

Chapter Four

Discovery

I'M NOW DRIVING A Suzuki Swift Turbo. Grabbed the latest version from an abandoned car lot. I must say I am spoiled. The car is quiet, powerful, and it's easier to swerve between the cars scattered down the many streets. The holiday home now is pimped to the max. The garage is full of cans, stored food, tools and water. The lounge has an 8k 80 inch TV, with 7.1 surround system just like home. A record collection now has a record player and the lounge suite and bed have all been upgraded to the latest store selection. I've started a garden at the side of the house. Containing any vegetable I could possibly grow. I'm quite proud of what I've achieved considering I don't have very green thumbs. YouTube has been my greenhouse council. I've spent the last few months searching each house one by one, leaving a black paint cross on each searched house or apartment. I haven't seen anyone or heard anything. The quiet is now driving me insane. I've decided the sighting of my wife was an illusion. A figment of my crazed mind. There's no other explanation.

The power died last night. Determined to find my wife, the thoughts about electricity and gas weren't important. Now I'm stuck in a black hole with useless appliances. A trip down to the local barn and I grab an array of cookers, torches, a diesel generator, batteries and such. I'm now heavily bearded, my hair is long. A little irrational, I'm wearing tough walking boots, a Hawaiian shirt and tiny shorts. It's the middle of summer. I'm tanned from being out in the sun and looking like a stunt double of Tom Hanks in *Cast Away*. *I must look crazy*, I think to myself. I catch myself in the mirror and start screaming, "Wilson!" Such a bad impression. I laugh at my forced comedy all the way to my sporty Swift.

Plugging the iPhone into the Swift, I look at the playlist to find something uplifting. My daughter's, 'Hey, hey calm down' playlist presents itself. I turn up the radio, put the playlist on shuffle and shove my foot down hard on the accelerator, the first song comes up. With the window down and the temperature outside reaching the high twenties, the song blasts out, echoing over the engine. *Xanadu!* By Olivia Newton John. *Fantastic,* I think to myself. A huge smile enjoys the breeze as tears get caught and carried into the back seat. What a choice! My daughter has picked the perfect song. I don't know the lyrics, but find myself ending each Xanadu as loud as I can. I haven't felt joy like this in a long time! Turning onto Main St, I'm about five minutes from the warehouse barn when I see something move. In my rear view mirror, I see a leg disappear back into a store. Like a body was being dragged backwards. I quickly pull to the left, park and hop out of the car. Straining my eyes, I see nothing. I don't like the look of the situation and decide it's time I was armed. 10 minutes later, I'm back from the warehouse barn with an AR-15 sport rifle. Loading it, I walk quietly up to the shop I saw the leg vanish into. I hug the wall and quickly look around the corner, trying to spot any villains looking my way. The shop is clear, empty but for the shelves still full of goods. This is a four square. A mini supermarket. Waiting a while, I walk in stealthily, sneaking to an aisle and crouching low to the ground. All seems quiet. Whoever was here has long gone. I grab a Moro bar, open the wrapper and devour it in a couple of bites. *Being a hero is hungry work,* I tell myself and laugh out loud at my stupid joke. The laugh cuts the silence and I hear movement. Behind the counter. I walk bent knee slowly to the aisle beside the counter. Grabbing a bag of peanuts, I chuck them to the other side of the store. Behind the counter, what looks like a little girl darts out the back door. "Wait!" I scream. "I mean no harm!" *Could it be?* I think to myself. I quickly jump the counter and push the back door open just in time to see a pair of shoes disappear under a table. I explained again, "I mean no harm, I'm a friend."

"Fuck you," said a little voice. I snicker at the rude reply. "It's okay." I say, "I'm looking for my daughter and wife. They've gone."

"No kidding," replied the voice.

"Look, I'm here to help." I'm now starting to think this girl doesn't want help.

"I don't need help," said the girl. "Take your pervy face, and piss off! Fuckhead!" she said with lots of gusto.

"Hey, hey, you're the first person I've seen in a long time," I say in a calming voice,

"You're welcome!" said the girl. I laugh again. I like her.

"Maybe we can help each other?" I said.

"You'd like that, wouldn't ya? I've done okay by myself," said the girl.

"Okay," I reply, "you don't want help? I understand, but something has happened that can't be explained. We need to stick together to get through this. It's dangerous out here, and you could use a friend," I implored.

"Bullshit," said the little girl. Just then, something smashed in the shop. I heard a scream, and what sounded like an argument. I turned to the little girl and said, "Shh, be quiet." Too late, she was already gone. I could see how she had survived by herself easily. She was a tough cookie. I peered behind the back door into the shop. Empty again. I hear a car start up, and speed off down the road. Looks like I'm not the last man on earth after all. I checked over the shop but no one was around. The little girl had disappeared. I leave a note for her on the counter with my address and name.

If you need help,
Michael Stevenson
13 Beach Road,
022342547,
your friend, fuckhead ☺.

It's as much a message to her as well as to anyone else who comes into the store. Now that I know there are more people around, it would be nice to have company. I grab another hero's Moro bar, and leave for home. *Xanadu* could be heard blaring as the Suzuki Swift disappeared into the distance.

Chapter Five

Shelby

I've almost searched the whole town now. Seen no one. I haven't come across the little girl, my wife, or the people who were fighting in the shop. My days are spent searching, and tending to the garden. At night, I've taken to teaching myself a musical instrument. At the moment, it's saxophone by candlelight. Now, if you're thinking 80s TV series, then you're bang on. I blast the quiet night with screeching notes. It's great for the lungs and totally out of my comfort zone. My wife would hate it. On this particular night I'm playing like my life depends on it.

I'm even working up a sweat. I'm about to hit the biggest, longest, wrongest note ever, in my loudest Hawaiian shirt when I hear that clicking noise again. I hadn't heard it since the car accident, when I thought it was my imagination. Six clicks, low and alien-like. Closer this time. Almost like it's outside. I'm starting to freak as they repeat. Louder still. I stop playing, put the sax down, and blow out the candles. In total darkness, I stand as still as a statue. About 10 minutes pass and nothing. Just the usual quiet. Then, as I'm about to move, six more loud clicks, like the noise is right next to me.

Fuck this, I think to myself as I sprint for the bathroom. I slam the door and lock it. I sit on the toilet, shaking like a leaf. I wait for more clicks as the shadows on the walls slowly move with the moon outside. I don't hear the clicks for the rest of the night. I wake up in the bath the next morning. I feel a little shameful when I walk apprehensively around the house. Everything seems fine, and the quiet morning sun is very welcoming. As I think to myself, *you're going nuts* and *what are you wor-*

rying about? I'm shaken by three large knocks at the front door. I slowly open the door and peer through the chain. "Hello, fuckhead!" said the little girl.

"How are you?" I say with way too much enthusiasm. "Nice to see you and welcome!" I'm bowing with excitement. She reminds me of my daughter and I'm so happy to have company!

"Calm down, Wakanda, I just thought I'd come and visit," says the girl with confidence.

"Calm down, Wakanda?" I repeat with laughter. "You're funny! What's your name?"

"Shelby, my friends call me Shell, but you can call me Shelby," she said with a sly wink. "Hey Mike, where are all your friends?"

"Mike?" I questioned. "Oh, that's right I left a note! I don't have any friends," I replied, feeling foolish.

"Don't be a douche!" said Shelby. "We both know there's no one left alive, apart from us, of course! Aye, fuckhead! Haha and you can call me Shell." Shell confidently walked into the house like she owned it. The house felt that much warmer.

Shelby is a breath of fresh air. She makes me laugh. So much so, that I forget about all the dramas we've had over the last year or so. She was living with her mum when everyone disappeared. Her father was never in the picture or didn't try to be, and hence she's always been weary of male figures. She's as tough as her exterior. For all her twelve years, she was cooking and cleaning, while her mum worked two jobs to pay the bills. You could tell Shelby was going to be something special as her character is just too damn loud not to be. She is built well for this new world, and I enjoy her cynicism and the false courage always on display. Some days I call her by my daughter's name but she doesn't mind. We've quickly become fast friends, who give each other shit, and enjoy each other's company. I told her about the clicking noise, and she said she'd also heard it, mostly at night. We both decided to dim the lights at night, and keep noise down to a minimum, as that seems to excite whatever it is making the noise. So far we haven't seen any animals or humans at all. Shelby loves to cook. We spend evenings working through cookbooks. I have a gas cooker set up, and we make some of the best foods I've ever tasted. In the morning, she makes me breakfast, during the day, I take her for trips into town or we work out in the garden. We read together and enjoy books at a feverish pace. Occasionally, she might exercise with me. Though she reminds me, 'I need it more than her.' I've come to consider her as family, and after a short time would be lost without her. One night, we were reading under candlelight, when she asked me. "Mike?"

"Yes, Shell?"

"Do you miss your daughter?"

"I do, Shell. I miss her terribly."

"Mike?"

"Yeah, Shell?"

"Thank you for looking after me," she said, with a huge smile.

"You're welcome, Shell," as I teared up, I reached over and gave her the biggest hug.

The next day was cloudy and dark. "It's my daughter's birthday tomorrow," I said sadly to Shell.

"Oh," said Shell, "how old would she have been?"

"Fifteen," I replied. An emptiness fell over the room. Both of us were silent. Just the noise of Shell stirring the eggs punctured the air.

"It was my birthday last week," Shell interrupted the silence. Whether or not it was her birthday, she instinctively wanted to take my mind off the weighted gloom. It worked.

"What?" I shouted. "No way! You're thirteen! A teenager, no less. We must celebrate!"

"Don't worry," said Shell. "We never celebrated birthdays. We had no money to spend." Shell looked at her eggs like they were the saddest sight on earth.

"Well in this world, we can do whatever we want, my girl!" I said, with joy in my voice. Shell knew what she was doing. My thoughts were now full of how I could make her happy. *Giving is the best gift,* I thought.

We raced around the Daytona racetrack on our twelfth lap. I had explained the weight-ratio problem to Shell, and she happily gave me a one lap lead. As she was smaller, her car could zip around corners, and was easily twice as fast. In this twelfth lap, she was pushing against my backside. Her evil smile could be seen flashing under her fogged up goggles. We were having the time of our lives. She faked to the right, which I fell for, before zipping down the left hand side to take the final lap. Did I let her win on her birthday? Hell no! I gave it my best! But like everything, Shell was built of sturdy stuff. We laughed, as we scoffed down our munchies taken from the Daytona shop. I sang happy birthday to her, and revealed a Harry Potter chocolate cake. She loved the cake. The *Harry Potter* series was one of her favourite reads. She said, "If this was a day in the life, she wished it would last forever!"

I said, that would be fine, as long as she'd let me win Daytona once in a while.

She replied, "No way! Fuckhead!"

We came back to the house, with the sun beating down on a breathless, hot afternoon. "Do you know what would be perfect?" said Shell.

"What?" I replied.

"A swim at the beach! We live so close, and I've never been."

"Well, Miss Shelby, your wish is my command! A swim it shall be!" I said.

"Mum never took me," said Shell, sadly. "You know, you're almost like the father I never had," said Shell, proudly. I pretended to look at the sky and beach in the distance. "Almost," laughed Shell.

Shell wore a Nirvana t-shirt and shorts, and I wore, what Shell said, were the worst togs in history! A multi-coloured, budgie smuggler, as she explained to me. Where she gets these terms from, I have no idea. Shell was making us some sandwiches, and I prepared the picnic basket. "Ouch," cried Shell.

"You, okay?" I asked.

"Yep, fine, just cut myself."

"Let's go!" I shouted. We hit the water with a running dive. It was warm, and inviting. I hadn't felt it this warm in a long time. No hint of waves, the water copied the colour of the sky, and looked like a beautiful photo.

"Man, how good is this?" I said.

"Perfection!" Answered Shell.

Funny, how the best of times can take you away from all the cares in the world. Just two people spending time together. I'd forgotten how wonderful it is to have a family. I smiled, as I dove deep into the water, and relaxed as the water enveloped me. I came up, and looked around to find Shell. She was drifting, slowly off in the distance, making a starfish. From above, she must have looked picturesque. I dove back under, and held my breath, enjoying the sunlight breaking through the water. It's been so long since I'd been in the ocean. Good on Shell for suggesting it. It was healing in so many ways. I came up again, and saw Shell was now further away in the distance. The tide had drifted her south, while she was doing her lazy starfish.

Just then, I saw it. A large fin piercing the water. It was a good 100m away, but abnormally large. Not like a shark's fin, more like a cross between a shark and something prehistoric. Another fin came quickly up beside it. Another fin? Or the same creature? *The same,* I thought, *they were working together.* My god, it's big and moving fast. I looked at Shell, starfish still working, ears beneath the waves. The large creature was on a pathway straight to her! I screamed and shouted. She didn't stir. *No, no, no, no, no,* I thought. I screamed, and smashed the water. Shell must have been almost asleep, while relaxing. The creature was 50 metres away now, and the fins had disappeared below the water. I dove into the water, and swam as fast as my aged body would let me. The rage of my strokes were all I could hear in my ears, as I swam faster than I ever had before. *No, no, no, no,* I repeated to myself, as I held my breath for what seemed way too long. I dared not look up, for I'd lose distance, but I quickly flashed my right eye, as I stroked through the water. Nothing could be made out, except a large shadow, up front. Shell or fish? I couldn't tell! I came up for air, and feverishly looked forward and around, but could see nothing, and no one. *No, no, no, no,* I thought. The water was moving, like a large boat had just passed, but I could see no sign of Shell or the creature. I swam in the area for an hour. Diving and searching.

Shell was gone.

I sat on the beach. Alone. Whimpering. My body was shaking. I think I was having a nervous breakdown. My Shell was gone. Taken from me. The girl that made me smile and laugh. She called me father. I cried out loud, and hammered the sand. "Fuck you!" I screamed. "Fuck you all! All of you! Fu...fu...fuck you all," I was shattered. My face was a mess. Crying, my vision was blurred. I then remembered, Shell had cut her finger. She was probably bleeding in the water. *You fool!* I thought. *You utter fool!* It's my fault. I shouldn't have let her swim. It's my fault! I screamed out to the quiet silence. Out of the corner of my hurting eyes, I saw my beautiful, blurred, teasing wife. Looking back at me, she walked off on a pathway, leading away from the beach. *Fine,* I thought. *Be here now.* Just when I can't see or do anything. I screamed again to whoever would hear me. Six, distant, unearthly clicks, answered my call.

Chapter Six

Sad days

The days move slowly by. I spend most of the time sleeping. I don't eat much, and over the last month, I have probably lost 20 pounds or so. I feel weak. The house is dark and musty. Everything is shut tight. The time moves from day to night, and for the most part, I sleep in the middle of the bed, face down. Thinking. Thinking about Shell. About my daughter. About my wife. Listening to the new sounds outside. More and more new alien noises. Not just the clicks but other strange sounds. It almost feels like I'm on another planet. I've locked the place down like a fortress. After seeing what was in the ocean my mind is now coming up with all sorts of scary visions to match each new noise. I've really lost the will. The will for anything. This is not like me. I really have been beaten down. My wife would be upset with me, I think. Shell and my daughter, disappointed. I'm nothing like what I was. I've lost all hope and all sense of reality. I miss Shell and her loudness. I miss her humour. Why couldn't I save her? I fall asleep again. A long sleep with dreams of my wife. She's leading me somewhere. Somewhere, familiar. Somewhere that looks like home.

Chapter Seven

Into the Trees

Two months have passed since Shell was taken. I made a little headstone out in the garden, where we used to work together. It reads,
Shelby,
2014 – 2027.
Taken from me.
A pain in the ass,
Miss you.

I'm feeling a little braver these days. I know my girls would want me to be strong, and to carry on. I've decided to go back home. The calendar I'd been marking off had long been forgotten, and I needed to update it. If there was a chance my wife or daughter had gone back home I needed to show them I was alive and well. Wife has not appeared of late. She only seems to turn up in dire situations. My thoughts are that she's a vision from a crazed, tortured mind. A mind that longs to have her back in my life. Without her, I'm lost.

I've packed an overnight bag. Closed everything, and made sure to leave in the early morning. The sea creature has made me weary of whatever is making those noises. Most sounds seem to occur at night. Driving quickly through the city streets, something seems different. A lot of the cars that were left in the centre lane are now gone. Moved to the side, and parked neatly or have completely disappeared. I've driven this route so many times each swerve and deviation has become second nature. Now it was a straight drive at high speed. Whoever was left with me on this quiet planet was a welcome neat freak!

Coming off the motorway, I drive past Whakitiki Forest on the left. Thriving with huge pines, an autumn mist sits on the top of the trees, creating a beautiful poster-like painting as I listen to The Veils, *Vicious Traditions*, powering out of the small speakers. Creating a dreamlike state travelling on the smooth road, it's like I'm floating by the trees. Out of the corner of my eye, I see something that looks like a large bear. But it stands still against the trees. Camouflaged by shadow, I'm not certain if it is or isn't my imagination. I peer in the left mirror of the car and see it looking at me. More human than bear but twice the size of a human. It stands frozen like a statue. I look in the rear view mirror, and see it move, fast and leaping into the forest. My head turns, and looks back in disbelief, trying to make sense of what I saw. Suddenly, something moves quickly to my left. In front of the car, I hear something huge and powerful. Faster than its size portrays. My head turns back to face the road but it is too late. The beast has ploughed into the front of my vehicle. The structure of my all too simple, cheaply put together, modern car is no match for the tonnage of raw power and my car turns into a vicious spin. My heart pounds as I let go of the wheel, trying to save my wrists and I pray the damage to my body will not be the death of me. The car falls into a dip, and then flies into the air, in what seems like milliseconds, I feel the seat belt jerk around my neck. Probably saving my life, as the car tumbles. It's abruptly stopped by a hundred-year-old oak tree. I taste blood in my mouth as my eyes start to close. The sound of the back wheels spinning wildly is all I hear as the last sight I see is the beast walking powerfully toward the car. It's half human, half beast like face, dripping saliva, and a row of sharp, large teeth, suddenly, brought forward in its mouth. It shakes its large mane, and screams a loud roar as my head pierces a headache. I lose consciousness, and my eyes start to close as I notice a blurry shape in the far distance that could only be my wife.

I wake to a warm dripping on my chin as I instantly feel a pain in my shoulder. *Nothing serious*, I think, and as I remember the accident, I thank the stars it's not worse. The seat belt is holding me in place with the car upside down and wrapped around the three metre width of the oak tree.

Shattered glass is all around me. I worry it's blood that's dripping from my lower body but upon tasting the liquid, realise it's oil. Oil that could quickly turn to flame if I don't get out quickly. The area is quiet, apart from noises in the forest. The sun is high, probably mid-afternoon. I see no sign of the immense creature that was scouting the vehicle. Again, I count myself lucky. The fact my driver's window is still intact probably saved my life. The passenger's side is smashed in. I try to push the seatbelt in when I hear the sound of a large breath. Followed by a snort. The sound is huge and bellowing. It's the beast. I hear its weight push against the underside of the car as what sounds like teeth rip into the back of the undercarriage. Easily opening the metal like it was a can of baked beans.

A breath from the beast that follows moves my hair as I realise it smells me and is trying to reach me by eating its way through the car. I feverishly push the seat belt button, but nothing happens as it seems the switch broke in the accident. The beast roars and the sound echoes through the car, hurting my ears as its front paws push against the opening trying to open it further. The paws work at different angles, powerfully, pulling the car from the oak tree. Again sending the car into a slow spin that propels it leisurely into the centre of the motorway. Walking at an uncaring pace, the beast follows the car. Its powerful paws hit the road as each step is followed by a sound that describes the weight. It lifts its heavy head, and again roars into the sky. My head looks to the sky as creatures that look like birds break from the oak tree fleeing the ferocious roar. The seatbelt is doing its job all too well as I reach for the glove box, hoping I've left a blade of some sort inside. The glove box thankfully opens easily as papers and pens fall out. *Never too late to write a note of last goodbyes,* I think to myself, *but not just yet.* I reach to the back of the glove box, straining with the tips of my fingers, finding a tennis ball and a small pocket knife. *The gods are with me today,* I think, as I quickly start working at the strap that saved my life. My eyes are darting at the seatbelt and the beast.

The beast is now standing with its hind legs, facing the back of my window. I notice its head looks back at me, and then turns and looks to the sky smelling the air. It's as if it knows I'm fighting for my life, and is giving me this time to try. Knowing it has bested me, I'd probably taste better if it lets me think I am free before viciously killing me. The knife is blunt, and I swear under my breath for choosing a knife that is useless. All the knives in the world to choose from and I choose a blunt one. I finally get to the end of the belts life and steady my fall with my left hand taking my weight against the ceiling of the car. Slowly letting myself down, I lie facing the driver's window as I notice the beast slowly start to turn. *My time is up*, I think. Its strength and speed is so awe-inspiring I really don't stand a chance. Then I remembered the tennis ball. Maybe I could distract it. I look behind me, and see the passenger window open. I grab the tennis ball in my hand, aim for the open space and throw with all my might. The ball bounces outside the car. As quiet as a mouse. It darts across the road and disappears into the dense forest growth. I look back at the beast. It's as if nothing happened. It snorts into the road, and moves closer to the window. *This is it,* I think. I've lived a good life. Behind me, I hear a scuffle. From across the road out of the bush comes flying a blur of fur and ears. It must be some sort of cat or rabbit, I couldn't tell. It speeds past the car, and disappears into the bush following the path of the tennis ball. Luck is still on my side as the beast bellows, and pounds past the car again, sending it into a spin which sets it upright, and adds more pain to my already bruised body. I know I don't have much time as I try to open the driver's door, which is now stuck. I bang my already sore shoulder against it. Once, twice, three times before finally the catch breaks, and I stumble out onto the road, feeling clumsy and out of shape. I stealthily walk behind the car watching for movement as I move to the back of the car. The boot thankfully opens first time, and I retrieve my gun. Feeling braver now, I back away from the car hoping to quickly find the next vehicle without being ripped apart. Another roar comes from the forest as I hear the beast coming toward the road. Trees are moving from side to side as the huge creature comes closer. I see no vehicle in close proximity, and decide my best chance to survive is to dart quickly into the dense forest.

Running through the forest, I check the road beside me, hoping to see a vehicle as I don't want to be caught out here in the night. My heart is pounding, and I feel more alive than I have in an age. I notice large tracks. Human-like but more rounded. My foot fits in it like a little child's. This thing is huge! The sun disappears under the dense growth, and light shadows guide my way. Sounds reminiscent of birds are coming from the tree tops but they are lower and louder. I can't quite see what these birds look like but I catch a shadow, flying high above. My god, it's magnificent! As big as a car, this thing lifts and shoots into the sky before disappearing out of sight. I catch glimpses of colour and feathers amongst the trees but they are well hidden. I've lost the bear tracks in my discovery of these birds, and now find myself lost. Forgetting where the road came from. A noise rings out in the forest. Loud and rumbling. Powerful and guttural. It is like belly thunder from something immense and powerful. I dive behind a tree, just in time, as a screaming creature comes out of the bush. Fearful of something chasing it, it darts this way and that like a deer escaping its hunter. Bounding at an unimaginable height, it leaps far into the distance. Just then, the huge bear-like animal I'd seen before comes out from behind me. I squeal at a high pitch that I'm not proud of as the bear pushes me to the side, leaps and catches the scared deer-like creature in its jaws. A sickening crunch is heard as its lock jaw closes and bones are broken. It stands over its prey, breathing and heaving after the powerful effort. The bush envelopes me as I quietly back away. *Snap!* I snap a twig and think to myself, *typical.* I turn and sprint as I hear the bear-like creature growl with fierce intent. I jump over logs and swerve between trees as I hear the bear-like creature getting closer and closer. It doesn't need to swerve. It runs straight through the forest growth. My heart is pumping through my chest as I realise it's faster than me and I will be dead if I don't think of something quickly. *My gun!* I remember. I could kill it. To the left, I notice a small cave-like drop into what could be a good hiding place. The creature is now on my back. Gun or hide? To be brave, or to be a scaredy cat? No time to think, I dive into the tunnel. I stop breathing and wait. The creature's noise and smell fly past me at a breathtaking pace. The forest is loud and rumbling as damage is left in its wake. I let out my breath as I realise it has covered my hiding place with falling greenery. *A good choice,* I think. I've run away to fight another day. I laugh to myself, and notice I've pissed myself with fear. *Dumbass!* I wait for a good hour, knowing the creature has now doubled back to get its previous hunt. I lift my head, and see the sun is late in the day. *Time to leave,* I think. I briskly walk back to the nearest open car, always checking behind me. I feel like a piece of prey, and vow never to be out in the open like that again. Finally finding an old pickup truck. I lock the car shut knowing the car wouldn't protect me from the creatures now in this world. What the hell is going on? Turning the key, I speed onto the motorway, as fast as the old pickup would take me.

Chapter Eight

Home Again

It's dark now. Late evening. I spent too much time in the forest, but finally returned to my home street. It's been months since I was here last. Getting closer to the main city, I notice the houses are deeply overgrown now. Bushes and grass are growing over fence lines. Houses are disappearing beneath weeds, and slowly the forest is taking over. Everything is growing so quickly it seems the human race will be well forgotten in the blink of an eye. I notice a lot more damage to houses and cars than out on the coastline. Windows are smashed in. Doors are broken. Some cars look like they've been stepped on. There's a feeling of unease, and the heavy metal I'm listening to is not helping. I turn off the radio and quietly drift into the driveway of 14 Lawrence Street. I sit in the car for a while as I notice the front door of the family home is ajar. All lights are dead in the street, and I can see varying shades of grey that make out the outlines of this once majestic house.

The front windows are smashed in. I'm not feeling so brave now. I weigh up whether to sit in the car and wait till morning or go in and investigate the house safe. If this were a movie, I'd just walk straight in. I sit for what seems like hours, but the cold and uncomfortable seat is pushing the balance to go inside. I've neither heard or seen anything, so I unlock the car. Quietly opening the door, I swing my bag onto my back and rest both hands on my rifle. With a tight, nervous grip, I start walking silently towards the door. The front of the rifle pushes the door further open as I peer into the darkness. It is hard to see anything, and takes too long for my eyes to adjust. The hallway is dark and long, and I can't make out anything.

I can't use the torch as I don't want to bring attention to myself. I close the door quietly, and my memory guides me through the darkness. I hear my body trembling in the dead silence as I move slowly up the stairs to the kitchen. *Calm, stay calm*, I tell myself.

Moonlight streams in through the shattered windows, giving me welcome vision. I see the fridge is open, and some of the chairs around the table have fallen onto their back. *Just the lounge, bathrooms, and bedrooms to check,* I think. Moving into the lounge, I see everything is in its place. The TV is still in good shape, and as I walk past I kiss my hand, and touch the screen. *My pride and joy,* I think to myself. I laugh a little as I quietly move into the master bedroom. The bed is unmade. Everything was left clean and tidy so somebody has been in it. Otherwise clear. I stare at the unmade bed for a long while trying to understand why it's messy. Visions of bear-like monsters sleeping in the bed crowd my brain before I shake my head back into awareness and move on. Walking like a special agent, I silently back down the hallway to bathroom number one. The door is open. I look around the door frame and notice a shadow in the corner. I strain my eyes and realise it's just a towel. Man, I'm shaky. I back into the hallway and hear something to my right. The sound is short and quick. *I wonder if it was me?* I carried on backwards down the hallway with my gun raised in front of me. I can feel my hands shaking with nerves. *Boom!* I fall backwards over the hall chest of drawers that has somehow fallen over into the centre of the hallway. The racket I make is loud and clumsy. I swear under my breath as I hear the horrible sound that makes my skin crawl.

Six unearthly low clicks. Turning over, and crawling down the hallway I enter my daughter's room. The window is smashed with curtains blowing in and out. The bed is still made. I was hoping it wouldn't be. Looking around the room, I see something moving in the corner.

"Fuck, fuck, fuck," I whisper to myself. I walk quietly over to the movement with the gun ready to explode. As my eyes adjust, I feel a sickness in my stomach as I lose my belly. In the corner looking like something from an expensive horror movie is a huge mass of small translucent eggs. Stuck together with what looks like black glue, the eggs are heaving and moving. Disgusting noises fill the air as inside I can see differing sizes of cellular growth. They look like small, vicious insects. I back away not wanting to see what will happen next. My mind is lost as I back straight into my daughter's desk and for the second time make a loud and clumsy noise. It echoes through the silence and this time, I hear the six loud clicks come from down the other end of the hallway. I raise myself, and slowly peer around the door frame's edge into the hallway. I see a huge, shadowy figure, impossibly covering every inch of the huge corridor. Its body is spindly with parts moving in impossible angles. Spikes are everywhere as the same black glue as seen on the eggs is dripping from its ugly body. I lose my breath as I move back into the bedroom and for the third time I back into something. My daughter's lamp hits the ground and smashes. I've stuffed it now. I make a quick decision to run for it. I speed out into the hallway. A massive squeal rings out deafening me as the huge creature is now moving at an alarming speed. I run as fast as my numb legs will carry me now running down the stairs to get to the main door. I turn and see the creature come into the stairwell, and crawl up the side of the wall and now onto the underside of the ceiling. "Holy shit!" I say to myself, as I turn, stumble, and sprint for the door. The creature smashes out one of the front windows, no doubt looking to cut my path out the front door. I raise my gun at the door, knowing this is probably my last stand. I will put all the energy I can muster from my wife, from my daughter, from dear Shelby into my finger twitching over the trigger. I back slowly from the door. I see the handle being pushed down, and steady myself. The handle is released, and the door stays closed. The handle is depressed a second time. The door starts to open. *Here we go,* I think. Before the horrible figure can enter the room, I shoot it! I hear it scream. I shoot it again! The creature screams again and falls. The darkness behind the door is all I see as I scream at the fallen figure. "Oh, yeah! Fuck you, you piece of shit! I got you! I got you!"

I walk up to the fallen foe. Feeling brave and strong. Preparing to feel horrible, at the sight of it, I wait for my eyes to adjust to its deathly glare. I fall to my knees. My eyes fill with tears.

"No, no, no, no," I whisper to myself, my voice hardly working. I look to the sky and scream. A long, painful, agonising wail. Looking down at the body. I see my beautiful, torn daughter. Blood filling her chest, and coming from her mouth. She gushes horrible breaths. Her eyes are open and wide, staring at me with both surprise and pain. Her hand grabs my arm as she stares at me. I cry and a tear rolls down her face.

"I'm sorry," I whisper pathetically, her hand slowly rises and tenderly touches my cheek.

"I love you," she says as her eyes slowly close. I scream again, looking up to the sky and my eyes come down and fall on the calendar sitting at the entranceway where I'd been ticking the days. On today's date, written in ink, are four words:

Dad, I'm alive! Lucy.

I am distraught! The new world has tricked me into killing my Lucy. I look about the dark house, seeing more than before. I see eggs now in corners not seen before. The house is foul and lost. The neighbourhood is probably the same. Smashed windows and doors are not done by the hands of humans. As I look at the face of my poor daughter, I hear the savage clicks once more. My gunshots probably scared off the foul beast, but not for long. Quickly, lifting Lucy softly, I carry her to the car, and lay her in the back seat. I found an extra can of petrol in the old pick up. I spray it over the entranceway till the can is empty. Lighting a match, I start a small flame that then erupts into life. I sit in the car, looking at the once-perfect home now lighting up the dark sky. The fire spreads quickly. Houses close by start to join in the dance of flame. I look back at my daughter, feeling worse than ever. I slam the steering wheel hard with my hands. After all this time hoping she was alive, how could this happen? I hate this new world and what it's done to me. First Shell and now Lucy. I notice Lucy is wearing a backpack. I take it off her and check for signs that would tell me her mother was alive. I feel a book. A scrapbook. The first page reads: Lucy's diary, end of the world.

I arrive back at the beach home. The sun is coming up, and all is quiet. The devastating ruin I'd just come from seems like a distant memory as the rolling sound of waves, and brine-smelling air quieten my alarmed heart. Lucy was alive and is now dead. I take my daughter inside and clean her up. All her questions are now quiet. Her enthusiasm for life lays silent in front of me.

A month has passed. I've laid Lucy to rest next to Shell. They can now question and give each other shit for the rest of their lives. I laugh. Lucy has a makeshift headstone like Shell, reading:

Lucy Stevenson.
Beautiful daughter of Michael and Teresa.
Forever in our hearts,
2012-2027.

I've been pretty down the last month. Killing your daughter will do that to you. I have food to last a lifetime, so I haven't needed to venture far from home. During the day, I'll sometimes walk the length of the beach. At night, I lock the house down and sit in the quiet dark. I sometimes hear noises in the distance, or I catch a blur of something in the sky I haven't seen before. The world is slowly changing, and my depression is missing it. On a particularly gloomy day, I finally found the will to sit and read Lucy's diary.

CHAPTER NINE

Lucy's Story

I'M SCARED. IT HAS been a month since I've seen my parents or anyone else apart from my kidnapper, this crazy, nut-bag, Joseph. He's nuts. Talking about the end of the world. About the problems of the world and how we brought this on ourselves. He's been slowly getting worse. He doesn't shower and stinks. I've never seen him brush his teeth or tidy the house. The place is gross just like him. He keeps me locked in my own room. Says it's for my protection. He's finally given me this book and a pen to write with. It's what I've been asking for as I'm slowly going crazy in this damp prison. The evil Joseph talks of monsters and how our time is up. How we can't leave the house, or we'll be killed. Once he even said eaten. He's losing it. Sitting in his own filth, reading his bible, and whispering things about judgement day and how the angels are making their choices. I miss my mum and dad. I've decided to write this diary in case someone finds it. In case my parents find it and I'm not around. It helps me to think. It gives me something to do.

I went for a jog when we were on holiday. It was early morning, Dad was still fast asleep, Mum was nowhere to be seen, and I suspect had already gone to the shop. I love my family and the life we have. I've always said it to them as an affirmation of what they have given me. Life is good! I did my usual routine of abs to start and then set out at a brisk pace. The warmth of the early morning sun was starting to mix with the chill breeze and I felt good. No one was on the street, and no cars were to be seen. *Strange*, I thought, but it is early. I turned the corner, racing into town. *This was going to be a new personal best!* I thought. I couldn't wait to tell Dad when I got back. I'm halfway through the beach city and I still haven't seen a single soul. *Weird*, I think to myself. Just then, an arm came out from nowhere and powerfully pulled me into a doorway. Strangling my neck, I was dragged up some stairs to an upper level. I struggled with all my might. It was like wrestling with a madman. He pushed me to the floor and his heavyweight laid on top of me. "Shut up!" he said. I can remember his individual stink even then. "Quiet, I say! You're not safe! The world has been cleansed, and we have survived!" I remember struggling and kicking him where it hurts. I managed to escape, but he pinned me again and the last I remember was his fist hitting my cheek hard as I lost consciousness.

I awoke tied to a chair. My wrists hurt, and my head was spinning. The room was unfamiliar, and it was the direct opposite of my dream about a family holiday before the smell brought me back to reality.

Joseph was sitting reading a book. Crunched up in a corner, swaying. He looked up at me with crazed eyes. "We are the only ones left," he hissed in a quiet voice. "Armageddon has become true. We have been chosen." He went quiet, licked his fingers, and turned the page on the book he was reading. I remember looking over the room. Posters of comics covered the walls. The house was a mess of clothes, and unwashed dishes. It was repulsive, and I wanted to leave. I remember a sense of terror and helplessness. He looked at me over his round glasses. His eyes, too big for the lenses. "You must stay with me. It is for your own good." I could hardly make out what he said next, but I think he repeated, "Yes, for your own good."

Great, he's talking to himself. I thought, this guy is nuts. I gotta get out.

A week had passed, and I was now locked in a small room. I had a bed and a desk. Joseph had brought me some clothes, he'd no doubt taken from a shop. I would put out old clothes to be washed but never got them back. Freshly stolen clothes would be left for me every so often. Food was cans of baked beans, vegetables or fruit. Nothing fresh. I asked for cereal, but it seems there's no milk. Joseph would disappear for hours on end. He'd come back and let me go to the toilet before telling me tales of noises he was hearing and monsters he'd seen. I don't believe him. I'm planning my escape. I must see Mum and Dad again.

The time I would make my escape had taken many months of planning. I was winning over Joseph's trust, almost to the point where he would let me go with him on errands. Today, we were going to the local four square to pick up some supplies. We had done this many times now, and he trusted me to stay quietly in place while he chose what we needed. While he was busy, I was going to knock him over the head with a tool from the shop, and make a run for it. I was fast and slim. He was short and fat. It would be no contest. We arrived at the four square, and as per usual I was the lookout for nothing in particular. As nothing ever happened. Today was different. Joseph called for me to take a bag full of cans with him to the car. As I grabbed the bag, I noticed a row of tools on the top shelf. On my way back, I would grab one and do the deed. I was nervous but confident.

There was nothing to lose. I placed the bag in the car's bonnet, and came back into the store ready to fight. As I came close to the tools I heard a motor far in the distance, and a song being played loud and echoing down the street. *Xanadu!* One of my favourite tunes! *Could it be?* I thought. I ran to the front of the store when I saw the vehicle speed past. In the front seat was a bearded figure. Dad! Singing, Dad! I jumped with excitement, and waved my arms screaming with my loudest voice. In my joy, I had forgotten about Joseph. He rushed to me and pulled me quickly back into the store. He dragged me backwards into one of the back rooms. We could see into the shop through a two way mirror. He had his hands tightly on my mouth to keep me quiet. I saw my dad walk in the shop! My heart was pounding. He was so close, and I couldn't say anything.

"Be quiet, or I'll kill him," Joseph whispered in my ear. Dad had a full beard. Blonded by the sun. He had a crazy, Hawaiian shirt on and the tiniest shorts. I was glad to see he had not lost his sense of humour. Oh, how I missed him, and his dad jokes.

Dad grabbed a chocolate bar, unwrapped it, and started to eat it. I laughed, and Joseph hit me in the back. Even in a hostile situation, my father makes me laugh. Dad's legs were tanned, and he had a rifle. Looking tense, I almost couldn't recognise him from the father I knew. He was checking out something by the counter. He chucked a bag of something at us before leaping over the counter and disappearing into the back of the shop.

"Don't say a word!" Joseph breathed into my ear. He pulled me into the shop. This was my chance. I grabbed a hammer as we passed the tools. But I slipped on the bag that Dad had thrown and missed what would have been a fatal blow. Joseph screamed at me, "You bitch!" As he hit my face hard. I punched him in the gut and screamed, "Dad!" Joseph hit me hard again and dragged me out of the store and into the car. This time, he punched me with full force, and I can't remember the drive home.

I'm taken out of the diary reading by a long series of shrill barks, far in the distance. The sound is ominous. I stare out the window for almost five minutes, waiting to hear more. Nothing happens. I look at the time, 4.30 pm. I remember the last passage Lucy wrote! What the fuck? I was in the store at the same time my Lucy was there with that asshole Joseph. She couldn't hit Joseph because of the peanuts I threw. Again, I've failed my kid. I curse myself for not having been brave enough to show myself. Someone really has it in for me. I remembered also that was the first day I met Shell. The first time she called me fuckhead! It's getting dark, I better carry on reading this tomorrow. A candlelight would be a sure sign that someone is home.

The next day, I wake and clean myself up before immediately settling down with the book. Lucy is a good writer, and I'm invigorated to hear what happens next.

It's been months now since I saw Dad. Joseph has become more and more irrational. He walks around the apartment, having conversations with himself. I can imagine him walking in circles. His protruding, hairy, naked stomach leading the way. He keeps mumbling about insects and noises in his head. He leaves for days on end. I know when the door opens that I'll be going hungry for a while. I've taken to saving food for when this happens. Preparing for the worst, I need to get out of here. Dad is on my mind more than ever. When I get out of here I'll go first to the holiday home. If Dad isn't there, I'll find my way home. Hopefully, I'll find him. I miss my family.

Joseph has not been home for four days. My rations are depleted. He's never been gone this long. I've been staring at my window now for weeks. It doesn't open, and there's a drop of three floors to the street below. Outside, I know every inch of the street. I've stared at it enough. I haven't seen whatever monsters Joseph has been talking about. The streets have been quiet and still. Then I saw her. Is it because I'm starved and weak? My mum is walking down the street! I scream to her. I bang aggressively against the window. She's walking in a slow come-what-may manner. Dressed in what looks like a long flowing dressing gown, barefoot, she lifts her head to the noise but does not acknowledge me.

"No!" I say, "Mum, it's me!"

Down below, I see movement. I hear clicking sounds and notice the worst sight I've ever seen in my life. A large, disgusting insect-like creature must have heard me, and disappeared into the building below me. I scream in shock. Mum, thankfully has long gone, but now I hear noises from the stairway. It's coming! Instinctively, I use my book and smash the window. Looking out, I see smooth timber running down the face of the building. There is nothing for me to grab. I'd never survive the jump. I hear the insect smash into the next room. A loud, disgusting, sniffing noise and the sound of too many feet. I have nowhere to run, nowhere to hide. I hear more footsteps and screaming. I look out the window, and think, *I have no choice. I must jump!* I close my eyes and... I hear Joseph! Swearing and attacking the creature. A large battle is taking place, and I can't see it. I hear slashing, cutting noises. I can't believe it, but I'm hoping Joseph will win. Furniture is being thrown against walls. I hear the loud, unmistakable bellow of Joseph's voice. "Die! You fuckin' hellspawn!"

Something smashes. I hear a heavy weight fall to the ground. Silence. I whisper to the door, "Joseph?" For what seems like hours, I hear nothing. Darkness falls, and something clicks by the door. Silence again. The handle turns. I move back. The door swings open with Joseph's hand attached. Joseph collapses from the effort in front of me. I look at the war scene displayed. Blood everywhere. Black goo dripping from the ceilings and walls, and in the middle of the room, the dead corpse of the huge, disgusting insect. A machete is in Joseph's right hand splashed in black gunk. His body is covered in cuts and bruises, and it looks like half of his face has been ripped apart. The insect lies without a head. Joseph had cut it off.

"End of the world I tell you," says Joseph quietly. He looks at me and then the creature. "I was just trying to protect you," Joseph looked back at me, smiled, took his last breath, and died.

I hated Joseph for the times he had me locked up like an animal. But I respected him for the fight he put up. He did this to save us. To save me. I spent the little time I could afford in memory of Joseph before packing a bag and leaving before any other monsters appeared.

2 pm. I've been reading my Lucy's diary now for most of the day. She was so brave and Joseph saved my daughter. I quickly ate some peaches from a can and then dove back into the diary.

I slept in an empty motel tonight. Chose the penthouse double room. I deserve it! Dad would be so proud. Feels so good to sleep in cleanish sheets. The shower works but is cold. Freezing. I soaped myself for at least half an hour. I think I was washing away everything that had happened. I looked in the mirror but didn't recognise the person staring back. I look older. Tomorrow I will make my way to the holiday home. Please be there, Dad.

I look up from the diary. Please be there, Dad? Where was I? Was I out at the other house? Surely, this must have been about the time Shell was with me, or after? I read quickly.

Have arrived at the holiday home. No one home. I looked inside, everything was locked, secure and tidy. The curtains were drawn. I left and came back four hours later before dark. Still the same. I'll come back in a week.

I look up again. That's it? That's how I always left the house if I was out. No, I must have just been out. I read again.

The motel is pretty cool. I swap from room to room. Have been reading plenty of books, and eating to my stomach's content. Have been to the holiday house twice now. Still no one there. The house always looks the same. Doesn't look like Dad's been there in a long time. Tomorrow I'll make my way to our home.

I look up from the book. Damn my tidiness, the house always looks the same. I had no idea. Why didn't she leave a note? She probably didn't think. I carry on.

Today, I grabbed a new mountain bike from the Cycle Triumph store. It is so smooth and easy to ride. I've ridden half the way to the house. I'm so unfit! My legs are sore, and I'm resting now in the

Imperial Hotel. Best of rooms. Much classier than my last motel. Had a bath as the hot water is still working! Heaven! ☺. Hearing noises outside, but have locked all doors and turned all lights out at night. Love you, Mum and Dad! See you soon!

A tear drops onto my cheek. Lucy is trying to find us. She's being so brave while being all alone. Reading her say I love you breaks my heart in two. If only I knew. I take a breath, knowing what is about to come.

Today, I arrived home at about 3 pm. The house is a mess. Everything is broken. The windows are all smashed in. I was so tired I slept in Mum and Dad's room. My room has a funny odour to it, and I left it straight away. Good news though! In the entrance, I spotted ticking on the large calendar. Someone's been counting the days. The last tick was a few months ago, but it means someone is alive! It must be Dad! I'll leave him a note on today's date.

Dad, I'm alive. Lucy.

I don't like it here. The house is too open. I don't feel safe. Will find a hotel and come back tomorrow.

PS: I just spotted Dad driving up the hill as I was riding down through the city centre looking for a hotel. I waved but he didn't see me. I'm racing back now to find him! Omg! So excited!

I look up. That's it. The last entry. She spotted me, but I missed her. It was probably near dark and I couldn't see her. She was coming home to find me, even at night. I feel miserable. Horrible. She was probably excited when she saw the car. Rushed to the door and was looking forward to seeing me. I slam the book. Close my eyes and cry. How could I carry on? My daughter is gone. The light of my life has been put out.

The last thing left on this earth is my wife. But does she even exist? My daughter has seen her too, so this confirms I'm not crazy. Why does she not acknowledge us? I must double my efforts and find her.

I need her more than ever.

Chapter Ten

In Search of Wife

I'M FEELING BUSHY TODAY. My hair and beard are overgrown, like the earth. Both have been fed at an accelerated rate. The beard is speckled with lots of white. Dry and unkempt dreadlocks are close. The earth is also unkept. Looking past my deck, the houses quickly disappear. Like the new animals roaming the earth, the plants are foreign to me. New flowers and trees make the planet look more and more alien.

An insect the size of a large drone drops and hovers in front of me! Six wings working in tandem protruding from its back. Looking more like a scorpion than dragonfly, its eyes look at me, trying to work me out. It blinks! I don't know whether to stay still or leg it? The huge monstrosity then turns and drifts towards the new fauna.

Two months have passed. I've searched the beachside town numerous times now with my sidekick, Pup. Still no sign of my ghostly wife. Why she's making this so difficult, I don't know. I sit on my deck looking out onto the main road. The early morning sun is trying hard to cut through, but it is more usual to live in mist and fog these days. I sit on an old-wooden chair, drinking a freshly brewed, rejuvenating coffee. I'm feeling more and more weathered. The last year has really taken its toll. Talking to myself has become the norm and I really am losing reasons to live on this strange Earth. Pup has been a godsend. He keeps me up, and his needs distract me from this strange world. His constant enthusiasm makes me laugh, and I love the days when we sit passing the time.

I pat him as he sits by me and watch his bum lift into the air. It never gets old. Today, I'm throwing a tennis ball out on the lawn for Pup to chase. He speeds out and picks it up in his mouth. Then like a helicopter, he flies back with his tongue hanging out. I swear if a dog could smile then he's doing it.

I look out onto the cracked and worn road, now filled with many weeds when Pup comes to life. He jumps to the edge of the porch, and is barking up a storm. I stand and look out. "Shh, Pup, what is it boy?" Pup won't stop and instead increases the volume of his barking directed to the right of the road. He's hesitant with his forward movement and seems to be going backward which can't be good. I crouch down beside Pup, trying to see what he sees while holding his neck. Pup's fur stands up on the back of his neck and his tails are upright. Then to the right, I hear a low growl. A muscular paw comes into view. Slowly walking into view is what must be the new king of the suburbs. Looking part-lion and part-bear, this huge predator is the size of a large truck. It moves with slow rhythm, sniffing the ground and surroundings no doubt for potential prey. It stops near an old Toyota sniffing the wheels before pushing its huge body against it, and easily denting the whole car. Its power and sheer size are immense. I remember to close my mouth after watching this creature in awe, and decide I could be the next order on the menu. I quietly pick up Pup, who is still barking and now trying to lick my face (God bless him), and walk back to the porch door. Not standing at my full height, my movements are slow and silent. The monster's snout is now sniffing the air to my left before its huge, powerful head tilts towards me and its eyes lock onto mine. "Fuck," I whisper to myself. Its head bows in readiness as a small high pitched whine comes with its next breath. Its large right hoof starts pawing the ground. *Goodbye world,* I think to myself, as I back into the house with my hand now firmly over Pup, acting as a muzzle. The creature's muscles are pulsating in readiness when, to its left, another animal of the same species enters the fray. Larger, if it is possible, than the first, it walks calmly towards its enemy. It's clear he's sizing up the other male for battle. Maybe, it's mating season, maybe he wants to eat me and it. Me? I'm just thankful I'm still alive. The larger animal is darker in colour. Its mane is huge and more pronounced. They move slowly, circling each other with low growls which echo through the silent streets. Coming from their muscular rounded bellies, the sounds are bassy and strong. Then they move. They are quicker than their size portrays. I would have had no chance. The larger animal is faster and quickly locks his jaw around the neck of the other. Cars are pushed out of the way as the scuffle is swayed left and right. They stand on their hind legs now making them impossibly tall. The muscles ripple as the front legs are used like arms, and they grapple with claws ripping flesh. The larger monster leaves the neck of his enemy, and tears at the nostril of the poor animal, taking a piece that now hangs painfully by a piece of bloody skin. I quickly move inside, locking the door. Running to the bathroom, I lock Pup inside, keeping his noise at a safe distance before taking a viewing spot from the front window.

The two powerful monsters are now circling again but it is clear the smaller bear-lion is damaged, and in pain, and wanting to leave. He whispers out an unconvincing growl and slowly walks back from where he came. *Wait a minute!* I thought. Whenever I've been in distress, whenever I've been in pain, I've seen my wife. First the car accident then Shell dying. Both times I was distraught. The same goes for Lucy. Something bad was about to happen, and she saw Mum. Maybe, just maybe I need to set myself up for disaster. I had an idea. A foolish one. But one that would surely bring her out of hiding. These monsters had inspired me. Tonight, I will light up the sky and finally see my wife or die trying!

Chapter Eleven

Companion

Day One

I came back today after a long search for my wife. 14 hours straight. Winding the long streets, and investigating each house and shop. Today's results were like every other day. Nothing. I sat in the empty lounge. The curtains closed and the lights out. The only sounds come from outside. My legs are tired and my feet hurt. I'm not hungry because I've taken a good amount of food with me, plus, I don't have the energy to cook or eat. The noises outside are becoming numerous and louder. In some ways, it is comforting to know I'm not alone. My eyes start to close as my fingers fall into the comfort of the armchair. A loud noise with a steady rhythm punctures the quiet. It grows steadily louder before ending with a booming bang, coming from the front door. My eyes open and my head turns looking at the door. The shadows are many and the dark is menacing as I wait for another sound. The silence is broken by the night noises again, growing at a steady pace. I rise walking quietly to the front door. Walking slowly, in case of alarm, I go to the front window. Pulling the curtain slightly to the side I look out and wait for my eyes to grow accustomed to the night. As my eyes begin to see, the shapes are familiar. Nothing seems out of place or alive. I close the curtain and turn to go back to the comfort of my seat. I accidentally bump into the table as pictures fall to the floor, making a loud noise. Outside, I hear scampering as something on the porch moves. I quickly look back out and catch a glimpse of what looks like a small creature. Possibly a small dog or cat. I pull my seat closer to the window and find myself drifting off to sleep. Every now and then, I wake to see if I can see anything. But whatever it was does not come back. I sleep long and dream of puppies and cats searching for my wife.

Day Two

I arrive home in disappointment. It is a long haul searching every house. It is soul destroying not seeing anyone every day. I close the curtains, and lock the doors. The house is dark again, and I sit in my seat by the front door with a small torch lighting my favourite read. It does not take long, whether it is a long passage of the book or just my tiredness, before I am asleep again. I am woken this time not by a loud bang but rather by my own loud snore. It was so loud I wondered if sleeping by the front door might not be such a good idea. I stand and yawn, thinking my own bed might be a better idea, when I hear what seems to be snoring outside. I quietly open the curtain to the side again, and see what seems to be a little puppy on the porch. Wrapped in its own warmth, its head curled in its legs. The night is quiet and I can definitely hear it snoring. I smile as I remember what dogs were like in a past life. This animal looks pretty normal, apart from a few extra bits. Mostly coming from the tail. I look at it for what seems like most of the night as its calm, peaceful sleep, and the rise and fall of its small tummy, feels like the most beautiful thing I'd seen in a long time. I decided to sit back in the chair. I listen to the puppy outside breathing heavily, and find myself nodding off to sleep. During the night, the only thing to be heard is a chorus of snoring between man and dog, keeping each other company.

Day Three

I arrived home a little earlier today. There is a skip in my step as I quickly unpack my bag once getting inside. Stopping at one of the numerous pet stores in town, I unpack a rather large eating bowl plus a huge bag of number one dog biscuits for puppies. The sun is just going down with a beautiful sunset as I lay the large bowl on the deck and fill it to bursting with the biscuits. I smile and look out at the perfect view while sipping back a nice craft beer. Feeling optimistic and hopeful I leave the door open and for the first time in a long time, make myself a home-cooked meal. The smells drift through the house and out the open door, hoping to catch a guest. The night comes quickly, and I've not seen any sign of my new puppy, which I've already named Pup. I close the door and lock down the house. Sitting in my chair, I don't feel as safe, knowing there's an open bowl of food on the other side of the door. Who knows what might come and eat it? I open the curtain, and watch the bowl like it's the most important thing in all the world. The sun wakes me as the warmth heats my face. My cheeks are red from bracing the window, and saliva has dripped from my mouth onto the window sill. I slowly stretch my broken old body before remembering the bowl.

I turn and look at the empty bowl. No sign of pup, but the food was eaten. I jump and salute the air. Pup likes the food! An hour later, I packed and hopped into my car, ready for another day. Driving off into the already hot day I leave behind the biggest bowl of dog food you'd ever seen.

Day Four

I came back in the evening to find the bowl empty and licked clean. I was enjoying my little job outside of looking for my wife. The job that is feeding Pup. I immediately rushed inside and grabbed the dog food plus a can of meat this time. Mixing it together, I thought Pup might need a little treat to keep him hanging around. I made another home cooked meal, my second in a row, and sat by the window, hoping to catch Pup eating. I was quite excited and hadn't felt this good in a long time. Not since Shelby was around giving me shit. I didn't need to wait long as out came Pup from the trees to the side of the house. He looked to both sides of the trees like someone crossing a pedestrian crossing and sniffed the air. His tongue came out like any normal dog and I could tell he could smell the meat. He then proceeded to walk along the pathway. Like a cute, little bulldog with his three tails swaying behind him. His walk was light and he carried himself with an air of confidence. He was white with black spots and had the biggest eyes. I must admit he was cute, and his eyes had an intelligence about them. Like all creatures in this world I've seen so far, he was built tough with two large canine teeth jutting out. He stopped just short of the porch and again sniffed the air before inspecting his surroundings. I could tell he couldn't resist the meat, and it was what probably drew him out so early. Pup decided it was safe and quickly popped up on the deck. His tails wagging as he made his way to the food. He looked left and right, and then stuck his face into the food. Eating happily, his tails wagged faster than ever. The three tails moved quickly almost like when a hummingbird flies. The three tails were moving so fast that they were a blur. Then the funniest thing happened. His hind legs started to come off the floor. He was so happy he was flying! I couldn't help it when I saw it, I let out a small laugh. Pup quickly came back down to earth and stood to attention. His tails dropped, and he looked left and right. He then darted off back behind the trees. Curse my loudness. I lost my little flying buddy! I put some more meat in his bowl to hopefully get Pup back, and sat looking out of the window once again. Unfortunately, in the morning, the bowl was still full.

Day Five

Came back after a long day of searching to a full bowl. No sign of Pup. Sat by the window all night. No sign of my little buddy. Woke up in the morning, and the bowl was still full. Left for another long day looking into the rear mirror.

Day Six

Came back home and the bowl was still full. Insects that looked like flies were everywhere. Quickly got rid of the old food and disappeared to the shops for a flycatcher. Tied up the fly paper, and filled Pups bowl with fresh meat, only this time, no biscuits. I was determined to get my Pup back. Sat by the window till 2 am, and then finally fell asleep. I awoke at 4 am to the familiar sound of Pup snoring. Wrapped up in his warmth with the bowl empty and licked clean. I slept like a baby.

Day Seven

Pup was gone again in the morning. I filled his bowl, and went out to carry on my work. No sign of wife again but came home with a nice doggy bed for Pup. As I locked the door for lights out, Pup came straight out from hiding. Ate his food, sniffed the doggy bed, walked around it like a cat kneading his bed, and then lay down with his head on the side. I had never been so happy. *I am the king of my castle with my dragon guarding it,* I thought. I punched the air silently and sat watching Pup before we both snored ourselves asleep.

Day Eight

Pup was gone again. Today, I left the door open. I brought his bowl, food and dog bed inside, and drove off for another hard day of searching with my eyes glued to the rear view mirror. Success! I came home to find the bowl empty and I'm pretty sure the dog bed slept in. I searched the house but found nothing. I daren't leave the door open at night, but Pup slept again on his dog bed and ate all his food outside the front door. He's a good dog. I'm very attached to my little buddy.

Day Nine

I moved the dog bed into the master bedroom with his food. Came home and the food was eaten. I sat by the window watching Pup tonight, wondering if I should invite him in. *Maybe I should show myself?* I thought. I looked through the window like a young boy looking at his favourite toy through a shop's window. I didn't even realise I was smiling. Suddenly, I heard a noise coming out from the trees. Pup was fast asleep. Two eyes glowing in the dark night shot out at me. I thought to myself, *lion or tiger?* It was low to the ground. I couldn't make it out. I rushed off my seat to grab my gun from my backpack. The noise must have been loud as it woke Pup and for the first time, I heard barking and a roar coming from the trees. I fumbled with my backpack and couldn't open the strap in the dark. Cursing myself, I tried ripping the bag, but it was too tough. Outside, I could hear paws running on the porch. The barking had turned to growling, and the roars had now turned to snarls. I finally worked the bag open, and tried to find my gun. I then realised I'd left it in the glove box in the car. I swore and ran to open the door without thinking of the dangers outside. The night was still, and there was no sign of Pup or the creature, save claw marks up and down the deck. I ran to the car and cursed myself again, as I left the keys in the house. Outside, I heard barking and what sounded like a fierce fight. A mighty battle was happening, and I couldn't help. After finally opening the car, I grabbed the gun and torch, and ran out into the night. The night was quite bright, lit by a full moon, and as a result was especially loud. I tried not to make too much noise but every now and then would let out a feeble cry of "Pup?" Knowing that the dog doesn't know his name but asking anyway. I searched around the property, but couldn't find anything. I started looking around the rear of the property and out towards the beach before deciding it was too dangerous. The noises ringing in the night were not normal, and too close for comfort. I turned to make my way back home when I walked into something big. It was lying on its side. I shone my torch on what looked like a large reptile with stripes. It had six legs and a body that was more like an insect. On the back of its tail was a large white stinger of some sort and the end of the stinger was missing. It was well dead and smelled of smoke. It was charred and looked black on one side. I kicked it feeling courageous and swore it moved. I jumped and ran for the house before seeing on his side looking very still, my little buddy, Pup. I knelt beside him, and saw no movement. I felt brave enough to put my ear to his chest, and heard his little heart beating fast.

I quickly picked up the little guy, and rushed back into the house, locking the door behind me.

Day Ten

I stayed home today and nursed Pup. By nursing, I mean, sat with him. He didn't move and slept all day. I placed his bowl of canned meat by him and placed him on his dog bed with a warm blanket. This time, I put some fresh water by him too. Why hadn't I done that before? I don't know.

Day Eleven

Pup is still sleeping. He hasn't eaten or drunk anything. I'm starting to get worried. I found a copy of *Lassie*, and put it on the big screen TV for him. It was too sad, and I couldn't finish it. Instead, I put *Babe* on and enjoyed it thoroughly. Don't know if Pup heard me laughing and singing.

Day Twelve

Pup still hasn't woken. His breathing is slight. My god, I think he's going to die. I just look at him all day. I can't think. I haven't eaten either or slept. My god, it's a bloody dog! I'm so tired.

Day Thirteen

I need to sleep. Pup has not moved but is still breathing, just. I've changed his blanket, food and water. I don't know but, I think it's only a matter of time. As the night closed in, I looked out the window. Nothing moved except the shadows. Slowly, my eyes grew heavy. I fell asleep.

Day Fourteen

I woke up with a weight on my legs. My eyes were stinging from a long sleep. I couldn't open them at first as they were held together by sleep crust. I rubbed them open, and quickly looked at the food bowl, empty and then the water bowl, empty. I then looked to see what the weight on my lap was. A smile filled my face as there, rolled up into a little ball, was Pup. Asleep on my lap. He was snoring as per usual. I lifted my hand and ran it across his side. Like a cat, a soft purr could be heard coming from the back of his throat. His eyes opened and almost as a reaction, he licked my hand. My eyes swelled with water.

"That'll do, Pup," I said, "that'll do."

Day Fifteen

Pup has become my awesome buddy! He's filled with energy. He eats a lot and loves a tummy rub. Only problem is, he starts flying when you rub him! So, you have to stop, so he comes back down again! Today, we stayed in the house, but tomorrow I might take him for a walk. He's the best.

Day Sixteen

Took Pup for a walk today. Things to note. He loves swimming. He's really fast. He's full of energy and won't stop moving. Don't make him too happy outside or he flies away!

Day Seventeen

I decided today that I should go out and start searching for my wife again. Thought it would be safer to leave Pup in the house. He whined as I left and pawed the door. Left in the car looking in the rear view mirror. Five minutes later, I came back home and stayed with Pup. It's too soon.

Day Eighteen

Today, I left Pup inside and went out to find my wife. Searched through five houses before Pup flew in through one of the windows. He licked me and wagged his tail. Came home to find a window broken. From now on, it looks like Pup's coming with me.

Day Nineteen

Pup is my Chewbacca. He sits in the front seat with me. He's handy, fast and alerts me of any danger. I never leave home without him. He now sleeps on my bed and keeps me company. He is this world's new man's best friend, and I love him. How can you fault a dog who is so happy that he flies all the time?

Today, we sat on the deck and watched the sun go down. I'm glad he found me because he just may have saved my life.

CHAPTER TWELVE

In the lap of the gods

I TAKE MY GUN everywhere with me now. Parking outside the warehouse barn, I investigate the car park and shop. No sign of life. I've upgraded the pickup truck to a Toyota Hilux Ute. Better suited for the terrain as these days it's like driving off road 24/7. Everything is silent apart from a strong wind. It's early in the day, I'm never out after three. I leave Pup in the front seat, lock the car, as I sprint silently across the car park and push the large doors open. Silence is the key to not being noticed or killed in this vicious new world. I crouch low into a corner, and wait to hear if anything is in the shop. No noise, no life. Walking quickly to the department I need to be, I fill a large shopping trolley with huge amounts of fireworks. All the good stuff and more. *Ah*, I think to myself, *tonight will go off with a bang!* Walking on this planet is like being a ticking time bomb. If I'm to die, it will be on my terms! I stealthily push the trolley through the shop, making sure to place a few treats in for Pup. I then sprint out to the car, load up the back of the Ute, throw Pup his treats, fire up the engine, and thank my lucky stars I've survived another outing.

The wind has calmed down as the sun sets over the holiday home's ocean views. *A fitting last sunset,* I think to myself. It has been a good day. I set up all the fireworks, looking out to the expanse of the beach.

My deck looks out to the garden of explosives. I drink a New Zealand Pilsner craft beer. Nothing has tasted better and the slight buzz makes me happy. I've seen no creatures to talk of today.

Tonight will hopefully be different. I sit on the old wooden beach chair, while Pup is sleeping a deep sleep on the deck. I think of past times. My wife laughing with me. My daughter doing her somersaults. Holidays from past years. Before I know it, six beers are sunk and I stop. The air is getting brisker. The sun has almost gone. My face turns from a smile to an aggressive stare. The battle has almost begun. My time here is short. I know that. Better to die a drunken hero, than a witless foe. I laugh at the sky. I laugh at the heavens. I raise the seventh beer I vowed not to drink and say, "Fuck you!" The beer is quickly drunk and I am ready.

An hour has passed in a minute, and it is now pitch black. All lights are off. I walk into the house. I look around one last time. Silence. "Tonight is my night," I say out loud. Pup follows me around the house like a shadow as I check everything over one last time. I take him into the master bedroom. We lay on the bed, and I pat him and watch him fall asleep. I'd already given him a hearty meal. Pup has been my constant companion and I wanted to keep him away from what was about to happen. This room wouldn't hold him for long, but if anything were to happen to Pup, I would not forgive myself. As he sleeps, I give him the biggest hug and watch his tails flicker. He snores a loud, familiar snore and I laugh as I give him one more final hug. A tear drops from my eye. I leave the room and my sleeping buddy, before locking the door and walking to the lounge. I walk over to the record player. It's already plugged into the generator. Everything is fired up. Noise is a good thing. I pick a record at random. Dave Dobbyn's, *Twist*. I laugh. One of my favourites. I pick what I decide is a fitting tune. I turn up the stereo as loud as it will go. The scratching from the needle signals my war cry. *In the Lap of the Gods* begins to play.

I race to the front of the house. Looking out to the ocean, I see no movement though as the night is dark. The song is playing loudly. I look at the fireworks, choose my first explosive and set it off. It is beautiful. The night sky lights up with a dance of sparks. First green, then blue, white and finally red. The rifle is ready on my right shoulder. I don't see or hear anything apart from Dave Dobbyn's electric guitar. I pick the next firework by size. Twenty small circles in one larger circle are lit by a single wick. This time white light shoots into the sky one at a time. I see movement. Out in the sea, a head rises from the water. With each bright light, it becomes bigger. By the end, I can see almost the whole body. Scales and teeth. An alligator of sorts but on steroids. Bigger, slower and scarier.

"Fuck me," I shout. "I'm going to die a gruesome death!"

I light the next firework. The song is now in full swing and I'm vibing to it.

"Better to die dancing than boring!" I confidently exclaim as I laugh to myself, another beer drunk. The firework illuminates the sky with red light. The beach is awash with a red glow, and my breath is taken away. I see multitudes of animals, monsters, insectoids and shapes. Nothing is what I could have imagined.

"Skal," I scream to the Gods, and drink the ninth beer empty. I light the next long, thin firework and it shoots out bombs of colour. Each colour increases the crowded beach. Each colour brings my death closer to me.

"Where are you, wife?!" I scream, "I am about to die! Come and see me! God damn you!"

I look out as the last yellow bomb of colour shows the first wave of monsters nearing the deck. The song is blasting out its outro. No sign of my wife. I look everywhere.

"So this is it!" I scream. "Time to die!"

I light the last firework, and it creates a blasting wall between me and the first wave of monsters. They hesitate before the brilliant light. The song is grinding out its last notes. I close my eyes and raise my arms. "Come and take me then!" The firework finishes. The song abruptly stops. I hear it. The sounds of the grotesque. Growls and moans. They come nearer. My arms and body spread out like a Nazarene crucifixion. I find myself starting to feel a little naked. One of my eyes slightly opens, I shout for the last time, "Wife?!"

As I see the open jaw and sharp teeth of the biggest, ugliest sea creature I have ever seen! It scares me to my senses. "Not today!" I shout at the horrific beast. I turn, and sprint back into the house with monsters of all sizes on my tail. I slam, and lock the door shut, and hear something big bang into the door. One hinge breaks loose. The door won't hold. I hear glass smash and in the darkness, see movement by the windows.

"Oh shit, shit, oh shit!" I whisper as I see shapes moving quickly in the darkness. I can't make out the shapes, and dive into the darkest corner of the room. My heart is beating through my chest and I wish it would shut up. I've royally stuffed this up. Why did my wife not come? She has turned up every time, but not today. The shapes are sniffing and biting objects in the room. As my eyes adjust, I see what looks like spiders the size of large dogs but with too many spikes and too many eyes. *I don't want to die,* I think to myself. The lounge is now full of them. Their movement is creepy and horrible as they crowd the room in search of prey. I run backwards trying to find the door before falling over in my panic. I try to get up, but feel the touch of a furry spider's leg as it is upon my ankle in an instant. I freeze as a group of the fowl creatures move around me, cutting any chance I had of exiting the room. My heart is beating loud. The creatures are surrounding me, watching me with their many eyes. Each one is waiting for the other to make the first move. I close my eyes and say a prayer, feeling the spider's leg moving up my thigh. I open my eyes to see its jaws leaking a stinking liquid. The creatures around me move forward.

"Where are you, wife? I am going to die!" I scream at the spiders.

Just then something smashes through the window. I strain my eyes to make it out. It's Pup! The spiders stop around me.

"No, Pup!" I scream, "Get out!"

Pup is barking at all the spiders. He is quickly surrounded but he is acting incredibly courageous. My buddy is trying to save me! The way to the door is now clear as the spiders are heading towards Pup. I stand and walk towards the door, watching the battle in front of me. Pup is trying his best to distract the spiders as one of the creatures moves towards him. It shoots out its claw, quickly catching Pup by surprise who lets out a loud yelp in pain.

"Pup no! Get out of here!" I scream again. I start to run over to Pup not caring of the danger when the strangest thing happened. Pup lowered his front legs and placed his mouth to the floor. His hind legs rose and with a precision like he had done this many times before, releases a stream of flames. From out of his mouth, a fire bursts out like a blow torch burning all the spiders within his radius. It is powerful and hot. It starts out as a small concentrated fire but then blows out to a magnificent size. He moves it from right to left, killing everything in his way.

"Fuck yeah, Pup!" I scream, and punch the air. Pup stops for a second and barks my way (God bless him) before spotting a second wave of scorpion-like creatures now forcing their way towards him. They are tougher, and he bellows down with extra force. Before I can help the second waves are upon me. I make for the door, feeling now that Pup could look after himself better than me and run for it. Down the hallway with the sounds of legs not too far behind. I turn into the bathroom and slam the door, locking it shut. I hear squeals, as something hits the door. The bathroom is dark with only a beam of moonlight illuminating the mirror. I look at myself. A wild man with a crazy Hawaiian shirt.

"You idiot!" I say to myself, "Now what?"

I hear scratching at the bathroom window. Everything falls silent. My eyes look bloodshot and tired. *Smash!* I have plaster and brick surrounding me as a claw bulldozers the wall and catches my neck. The power and strength of the claw squeezes my all too human neck as I look at the eye of what I now know is my killer. Like the eye of a lobster, it stares at me as I feel the pincers start to close. Instinctively, my left arm springs into action, grabbing my machete from my back and slicing the eye clean off. The claw releases me. Giving me enough time for my right hand to aim and fire the rifle clean into its brain. Feeling brave, I sprint for the bathroom door. I open it, pushing large scorpions behind it with their tails searching for me, and make for the garage. I turn, and spray a fire of bullets at all monsters making their way towards me before opening the garage door and slamming it shut behind me.

Chapter Thirteen

The Last Stand

My breath is racing. My heart is pounding. *How the fuck did I do that?* I think to myself. My mind has thoughts of Pup making his stand. I can hear him barking in the distance, and what sounds like streams of fire being let loose. The house is hot, and probably in flames where Pup is. I shake my head, thinking about Pup's new power. Actually, he's probably had it all along as I remembered the charred creature he must have killed when we first met. I look around the garage. Not much food left. It is huge and empty. The double doors in front of me carry windows at the top that look out into the cold night. I hear noises of monsters trying to get in at both entrances. I can hear fights going on and strange things getting eaten. They are killing each other while trying to get to me. The doors won't hold. What do I do now? Pray? I sit in silence. Rifle at the ready sitting in the dark corner. A beam of light places a couple of light breaks across my eyes. My last chance. My last stand is to take it outside to the street. Die a man, fighting with Pup. My wife, Lucy and Shell would be happy! Proud! Then I will be merry, and eat with them and Pup in Valhalla! *Too much TV,* I think to myself.

I check my rifle making sure it is fully loaded. Machete at the ready. I stand at the double doors, ready to fight, ready to battle. I close my eyes, and say one prayer to whoever will listen. I look at the doors. My stare is angry. I want to live now. More than ever. I move towards the garage door chain. I start to draw the chain toward me. Underneath the door, I can hear the noises and smells of beasts.

A huge nostril sniffs the ground and my feet draw back. The chain is still working. I feel my destiny is upon me when a light, a beautiful, bright light appears to the right through the windows of the double garage door. I back away, shielding my eyes. It drifts from right to left. Slowly, but steadily. The room's light moves with it. I move further back and take it in. Outside, the noise goes silent. Behind me, the monsters are quiet. The light hovers to the left, and is still behind the entrance door. The handle turns.

"What the fuck?" I whisper.

I point the rifle at the door. The door opens, and the light fills the room. This time, I hold my rifle shot. Standing in the doorway is my beautiful wife, Teresa! She is an angel. In flowing gowns, pure light and barefoot, like Lucy described. I kneel and cry. Tears come pouring like I've never felt before.

"Teresa!" I scream.

"No, I am not Teresa," said the being. Her voice was unearthly but distinctly Teresa's in timber. My tears stop, my rifle points at her.

"Then who are you?"

"I am whoever you want me to be, Michael Stevenson." I looked stunned and questioned, "What does that even mean?"

"I am not who you remember nor anything you can understand, Michael Stevenson," it said in a calming voice. "We have been here for many millennia, and will be for many more."

I set my rifle down and remembered the hordes outside.

"Ah, the door is open, you might want to close it."

"The creatures that surround us will not trouble us while I am here."

Somehow, I believed her as I sat in astonishment. It was quiet for an eternity while I thought on my next question. She answered before I could say anything meaningful.

"Why am I here? We have been custodians of this planet. We birthed it, and made it what it is. This world you call Earth is one of many. It is for us to decide what lives on it. We select it and breed it. The planet decides what lives and what dies. If the planet is dying, we step in, Michael Stevenson."

"You step in?" I say quietly.

"Yes, we have done so many times with what you call the dinosaurs, and before them, the Acrimaycs, before them, the wonderful architects that were the Midotarians, and before them, still, the Hotterics, those who were bathed in flame! All have been selected for extinction. As you humans have been, their lives were more important than the Earth's. I can see you are in shock. I understand."

Silence reigns as her head looks into space and gathers her thoughts.

"All humans were meant to be vanished, Michael. Some survived. I and the animals birthed anew are here to make sure of it."

I am quiet. The more I am silent, the more it tells me.

"To make sure of it?" I ask.

"I appear to those who survive as a form of comfort. The last sight before they are supposed to die,

Michael. You have not died yet, and I do not know why."

"I don't want to die," I speak sternly to the being, "I, my...my family have been taken from me!" I look at her with a tear in my eye. "Can you bring them back?"

"Bring them back? Michael Stevenson, I am supposed to be rid of you." She paused, and looked at me. Looking like something from an old religious picture, she whispered to me with outstretched arms. "I am intrigued by you, Michael. You have survived, and have fought for your family. You love them with a fierceness I have not seen in any animal before." She paused, and looked away in thought, then turning back she said, "I have spoken with those who will listen. We wish to give you a second chance."

I look at her with a fresh look of hope.

"A second chance?"

"Michael?" Behind me, out of nowhere, stood my wife Teresa in the same clothes I'd last seen her in.

"Teresa?" My eyes flooded with emotion, and I gave my wife the biggest hug I could muster. My arms held her tightly, and I felt like I'd never let go. I kissed her cheek repeatedly before doing the same to her forehead. "I've missed you! I've missed you so much!"

Teresa was smiling, if a little lost with the whole situation. She looked at the being in front of us. "Who's the looker?" said Teresa.

"Dad?" I turned quickly and fell again to my knees.

"Lucy? Lucy, Lucy!" I ran to my daughter and again grabbed her into a mighty hug. "I'm so sorry, Lucy," I said with pain in my voice. "It was a mistake, I thought you were the creature!" I held her shoulders as mad tears were now coming down in buckets. I was so happy to have them both back.

"Hey fuckhead!"

"Oh my God," I proclaimed as my face showed even more surprise. I looked behind Teresa, and there angling to the side with a huge cheeky grin was Shelby! "Can't get rid of me!" I ran over and picked her up off the ground.

"I'm so sorry!" I said, "I tried to get to you."

"It's okay," said Shelby, "I'm here now!" She hugged me back, got up on her tippy toes and kissed my cheek. Shelby looked at me inquisitively and asked, "Are you going to introduce me?" She didn't wait for an answer, walking up to Lucy. "Hi, my name's Shelby, my friends call me Shell, but you can call me Shelby!" She looked at me with a wink. She looked back at Lucy, "What's your story?"

Lucy answered with a smile. "Oh, my story's nothing special. Just, my Dad killed me!"

"Oh shot!" said Shelby, "I died on his watch also!" I look away from the smartasses and catch Teresa's stunned face. Her mouth is wide open, aghast, at what the girls have just said. Her shocked face slowly breaks down any faith she had in me.

"They exaggerate!" I said, with shoulders shrugging. I held them close together, already feeling like a happy family, when I remembered the being.

We all looked at her. She spoke slowly and calmly, "You have a second chance. Something not given before. Do not take it lightly. You will probably not survive, Michael Stevenson. My council and I bid you hope. May you prove our last selection wrong." She smiled at the family before turning and walking slowly towards the door.

I grabbed my family and told them to follow quickly. We stayed within the being's light, before entering the Toyota Ute. Shelby screamed out, "Shotgun!"

Before Teresa answered, "Not on your life!" And jumped in the front seat.

Shell and Lucy instead grabbed the back. The being in light, slowly walked away, looking at the animals moving out of her way as if they were her children. We all looked at her mesmerised. As the light slowly disappeared, I remembered the monsters ready to kill me and now my family. Before we could move, a huge monstrosity of an animal came charging towards the car. The light from the being no longer protecting us. We were fair game. I hadn't had time to put the keys in, and in true form couldn't remember which pocket I'd put them in.

"Ah, Dad?" said Lucy, as the monster charged closer.

I turned and watched, as the monster lowered its head like a dinosaur from another age. Checking all my pockets, I couldn't find the keys and swore under my breath.

"Fuck me and my ignorance!"

Shelby looked at me and calmly said, "Swearing!"

The monster was seconds away, when I remembered I put a spare set above the visor.

"Too late!" Screamed Shelby when, out of the blue to the left of the car came a large stream of fire. It was a massive display of flame and it turned the massive beast to its side, narrowly missing the car.

"Pup!" I screamed and punched the air.

"Who?" said Teresa. Out of the darkness, to the left of the car came a sight for sore eyes. Pup was barking up a storm and actually made the surrounding monsters retreat in fear. He let out a huge stream of fire that covered the driveway and lit up the waiting monstrosities in all directions. As quick as he had appeared, he stopped the flame, turned, and sat like a good dog wagging his tails with his tongue out, looking at all of us staring at him with our faces pressed against the windows.

"Oh, so cute!" said Lucy.

"Can we keep him?!" said Shell.

"What are you talking about? That's my dog!" I shouted proudly. I winded down Lucy's back window using the power switch from my side, and screamed out. "C'mon Pup, you good thing!" Immediately, Pup's tails started whirling and his hind legs rose up into the air.

"Oh my gosh, that is so cool!" said Shell.

Pup raised himself into the sky, and floated neatly into Lucy's window, sitting comfortably between Lucy and Shell.

"Oh my God, he's adorable!" said Lucy with hands raised to her mouth.

Both Shelby and Lucy started patting Pup, who seemed quite in heaven, his tails lifting him up to the ceiling of the car and down again. "You're cleaning up the poop," said Teresa.

"So we can keep him then?" I said with a smile.

"Of course," said Shelby, with a wink as Teresa looked back with a smile. I finally started the car, turned on the lights, and quickly swerved onto the road. Powering through the few beasts that were in the way, the car shot out onto the motorway, swerving between stationary cars. Teresa looked at me.

"What just happened?"

"I know, I will explain!" I smiled at her and the girls. "I've got you all back, and we've been given a second chance." My hand rested on my wife's shoulder. "I promise, we're gonna make it!"

"Like last time?" smiled Shelby,

"No," said Lucy. "This time, Dad's got his family."

As we drove off onto the dark motorway, I checked the rear view mirror, and smiled as Pup looked at me. His tails spinning while he floated in the air being patted by Shelby and Lucy. He barked at me, as happy as I had ever seen him.

I grabbed Teresa's hand, and smiled. This world was tough but with my family, I felt even tougher.

Thank you for reading *A Day in the Life*.
Please share your feedback on social media using our hashtags and handles:*#Adayinthelifebookseries*

Join the review team family and receive a free advanced copy of the next book in the series.
Join the mailing list, place in subject: Review team. please visit: *www.andrewmasseurs.com*

To get the latest news, join the mailing list and for additional resources,
or to book *Andrew Masseurs* to speak at your event please visit: *www.andrewmasseurs.com*

If you enjoyed this book, please consider writing a review with your honest impressions on Amazon, Goodreads,
or the platform of your choosing.

Your feedback is incredibly valuable for helping independent authors like us reach a wider audience.

Made in the USA
Columbia, SC
24 June 2024